REMEMBER BETSY FLOSS
and Other
Colonial American Riddles

REMEMBER BETSY FLOSS

and Other Colonial American Riddles

David A. Adler

illustrated by
John Wallner

Holiday House / New York

For my nephew Sol
D.A.A.

For David Rogers
J.C.W.

Library of Congress Cataloging-in-Publication Data

Adler, David A.
  Remember Betsy Floss

  Summary: An illustrated collection of humorous
riddles about American colonial life and the
Revolution.   1. Riddles, Juvenile.   2. United States—History—
Colonial period, ca. 1600–1775—Juvenile humor.
3. United States—History—Revolution, 1775–1783—
Juvenile humor. [1. Riddles.   2. United States—
History—Colonial period, ca. 1600–1775—Wit and
humor.   3. United States—History—Revolution,
1775–1783—Wit and humor]   I. Wallner, John C.,
ill.   II. Title.
PN6371.5.A3229   1987   818'.5402   87-45333
ISBN 0-8234-0664-4

Who was given thread to sew a flag but cleaned her teeth instead?

Betsy Floss.

What's big, cracked and wiggles?

The Liberty Jell.

Did George Washington catch his men drinking ale?

No. He caught them with their pints down.

How were George Washington's wigs delivered?

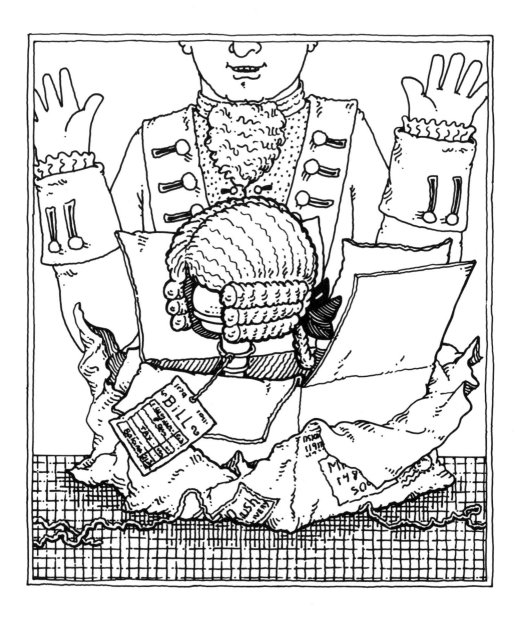

By hair mail.

How did Dolly Madison make a jelly roll?

She pushed the jar off the table.

How long did Benjamin Franklin's candles burn?

About a wick.

At dinner, would John Paul Jones pass the salad?

Yes. But he wouldn't give up the dip.

What's red, white and blue?

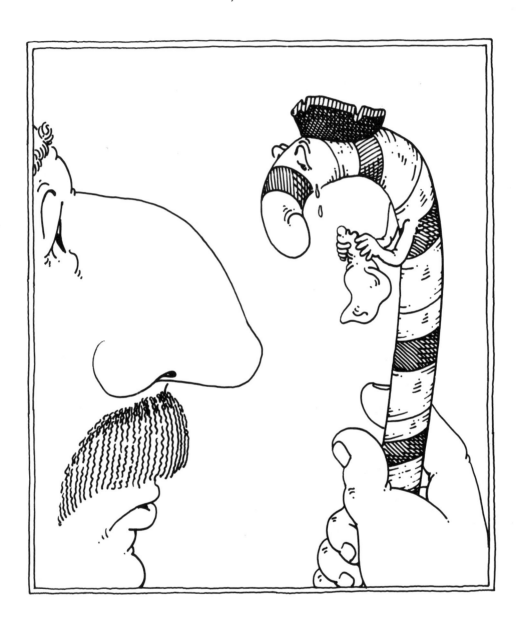

A sad peppermint stick.

What did the flag say to Thomas Jefferson?

Nothing. It just waved.

What do you call the hearts and flowers on a man's shorts?

The decoration of underpants.

What did Betsy Ross say when her flag ripped?

"Darn it."

How do you know Plymouth Rock is made of stone?

I just took it for granite.

What do sixty minutemen make?

An hour, man!

What did Paul Revere say at the end of his famous ride?

"Whoa!"

What's red, white and blue and bad for your teeth?

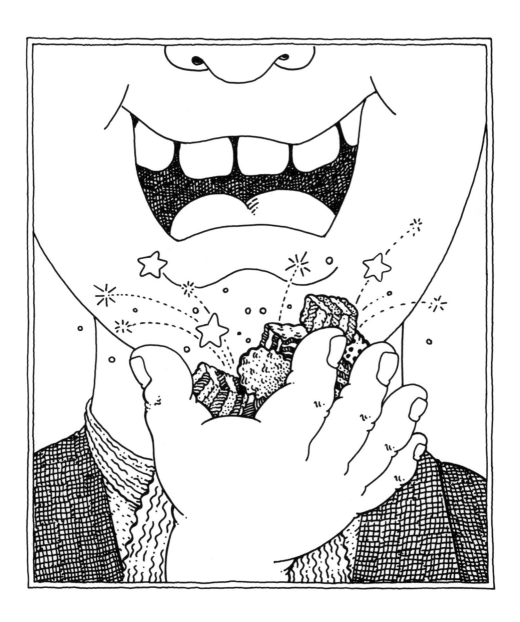

Yankee Doodle Candy.

Did George Washington fight bear?

No. He fought dressed.

How did Betsy Ross like her work?

Sew, sew.

What's the difference between Paul Revere's horse and his duck?

One went quick. The other went quack.

Why did the minutemen stop on Main Street?

To salute the general store.

What did the colonists do about the sugar tax?

They raised cane.

What's the difference between President Washington and an old shoe?

One was sworn in and the other was worn out.

Did Thomas Jefferson make his own coffee?

No. It was too much of a grind.

What did people say when Yankee Doodle rode by on a toy horse?

"Yankee Doodle went to town riding on a phony."

Why did Washington's soldiers stop fighting in trenches?

They were sick of the hole business.

What did George Washington do when his ax broke?

He put a new one on his chopping list.

Why did Benjamin Franklin fly his kite?

He got a charge out of it.

What did George Washington do when his ax broke?

He put a new one on his chopping list.

Why did Benjamin Franklin fly his kite?

He got a charge out of it.

What's red, white, blue and sneezy?

Uncle Sam with a cold.

What had two heads, six feet and rode through Boston yelling "The British are coming?"

Paul Revere and his horse.

Why were George Washington's teeth like the stars in the sky?

They came out at night.

What did George Washington say when he dropped his false teeth?

"Head for the hills, men. The bridge is out."

Who made the puddle on the Boston Post Road?

The town crier.

What did the drummer boys of the Revolution do in the winter?

They played it cool.

Which hero of the Revolutionary War slept with his shoes on?

Paul Revere's horse.

What was the colonists' favorite tea?

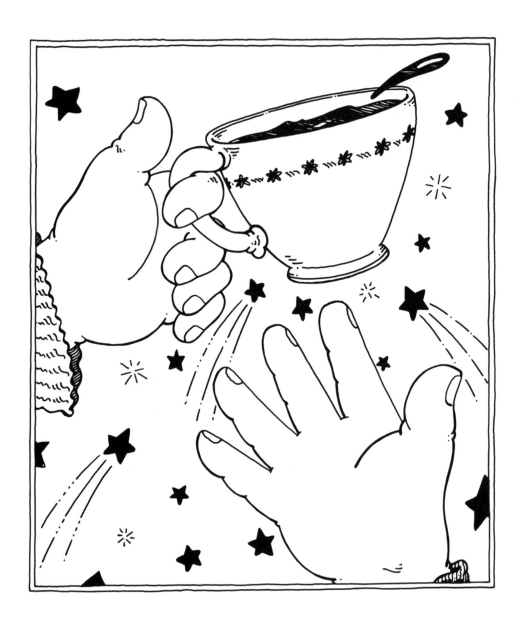

Liberty.

How were a Redcoat soldier and a salted peanut alike?

They both were shelled.

Did Sam Adams ever sleep on plastic sheets?

Sure. In his vinyl resting place.

When Betsy Ross washed the flag, why did she add starch?

She wanted a permanent wave.

Did anyone make a speech on the Mayflower about cotton shorts?

Sure. It was the deck oration of underpants.

What did Benjamin Franklin overlook?

His nose.

How did Benjamin Franklin feel when he discovered electricity?

Shocked.

What's a fancy dog called in Boston?

A Yankee Poodle Dandy.

What did Thomas Paine's teacher have?

A pain in the class.

How did Paul Revere drive his horse buggy?

He tickled it.

Where was the Declaration of Independence signed?

On the bottom.

Why was the stamp tax like a peppermint stick?

They both had to be licked.

When is a piece of wood like King George III?

When the piece of wood is a ruler.

Why didn't George Washington need a bed?

He wouldn't lie.

Why were Washington's soldiers so tired on the first of April?

They just had a March of thirty-one days.

Why is a healthy horse like the United States?

They both have a good constitution.

What happened to the boots the Redcoats wore?

They went down to defeat (the feet).

Which vegetable wasn't allowed on the Mayflower?

The leek.

Which American had the most children?

George Washington. He was the father of the country.

Why was Paul Revere's horse like a bad dream?

It was a nightmare.

Why was Paul Revere sent home from school?

For horsing around.

Why can so few Indian couples relax?

They are two in tents (too intense).

Why did the Pilgrims bring two drums and a saxophone on the Mayflower?

They wanted to see Plymouth Rock.

What did the Pilgrims say after they had been in America for a while?

"Long time no sea."

What did the innkeeper tell George Washington when he asked for beds for his men?

"That's a lot of bunk."

How is the Liberty Bell like a wooden apple?

They both can't be pealed (peeled).

What was Ben Franklin's kite made of?

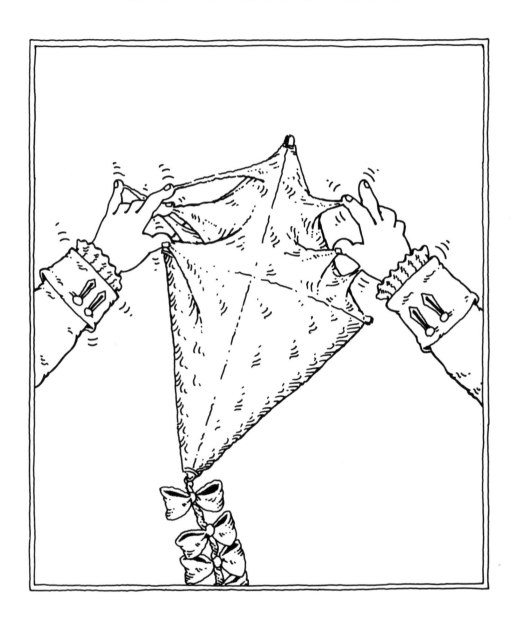

Flypaper.